·L·A·C·E·Y·

Illustrated by Linda Voight

Library of Congress Cataloging-in-Publication Data

Fattah, Michel.
    Lacey.

    1. Divorce—Fiction. 2. Dogs—Fiction.
I. Title.
PZ7.F2684Lac.   1990   [E]   89-62244
ISBN 0-915677-47-4

First Edition

10   9   8   7   6   5   4   3   2   1

· L · A · C · E · Y ·

My Life As A Toy Poodle

As Told To

MICHEL FATTAH

Illustrated By Linda Voight

ROUNDTABLE PUBLISHING, INC.
933 Pico Blvd.
Santa Monica, CA 90405

Hello. My name is Lacey and I'd like to be your friend. I'm a white toy poodle. When I was very young I shared a tiny room with two friends at the pet store, and we had lots and lots of fun playing with each other. There was a parrot there that greeted the customers and put everyone in a good mood.

One day a lady stopped and smiled at us. It made me so happy
when she picked me up and nuzzled my face. So I gave her a
kiss. "Aren't you wonderful," she said. "So soft and pretty. Your
fur is just like lace, and that is what I will name you. Lacey!"
Well, that sounded nice and made me feel happy.

When we started away from my friends I didn't know what to think. Then she put me down and I got frightened because I thought I was all alone. I missed my friends and the world seemed so big. It was pretty scary. But I needn't have worried. The nice lady quickly picked me up again and we left the store.

She carried me a long, long way. Then she put me into another
room and she sat beside me and took hold of a big wheel. And
the room moved! Well, I protested with an "arf! arf!" I was in
a car for the first time, you see. The pretty lady laughed and held
me while she drove. I knew everything was going to be fine.

8

Soon we got to this house by the sea. It was my new home and
a little girl named Nancy also lived there. She was the daughter
of Mrs. Clark, the lady who'd taken me from the store. It was
exciting, exploring the house and being the new baby in the
family. That was what my new Mommy told Nancy I was.

There were wonderful new things to look at and lots of rooms
to explore. Of course the room I liked best was the kitchen
because it smelled of food. Best of all, pretty sailboats floated
past the huge window that looked out on the sea. I tried to say
hello to the people on them but I guess they couldn't hear me.

Soon I was in for another surprise. A Daddy! He came home
bringing all sorts of new toys. There were squeaky toys and
chewy toys and, best of all, a big round ball. I was exhausted
from playing when it came time for bed. Still, I missed my
friends a little bit and cried, until Nancy tucked me in.

I was up early the next morning! What a sleepy head Nancy
turned out to be. However, she had to go to school and I missed
her. Then Daddy showed me a special game called "go fetch."
He'd throw the ball across the polished wood floor and I'd
chase after it and push it under the china cabinet with my nose.

Then I made a wonderful discovery! When Daddy would bend down to get the ball from beneath the furniture, I could kiss him right on the nose. Oh, that was fun and Daddy laughed so hard that Mommy came in from the kitchen to see what was going on. She thought it was funny, too, and rubbed my tummy.

Christmas came only a few days after I came to live with
Mommy, Daddy and Nancy. What a surprise! I got a very special
present. It was wrapped in a large box and they let me open it
myself. I didn't think anything could be so much fun as ripping off
the pretty paper with my teeth. But then I saw something inside!

14

I really didn't know what it was at first. It was a big thing, bigger than I was. It also had soft fur. At first I thought it was another new baby and felt a little bit jealous. Then Mommy told me it was a "teddy bear" and Nancy said his name was Mr. Bear. And that he was going to be my new friend!

Mr. Bear was fun to play with. I spent Christmas day showing him about, dragging him from room to room. That night I tried to take him to bed but he was just too big for me to jump that high with. Nancy thought that was funny. She helped me and we had a new companion to visit dreamland with...

Everything seemed so perfect. I was forever running about the house with Mr. Bear in my mouth and crashing into walls and making Mommy, Daddy and Nancy laugh. They all agreed that we were a very funny pair. Nancy said she thought we should be on television. It's hard work, keeping your family amused.

Then one day I noticed that Mommy wasn't laughing at us anymore. I quickly ran and got the ball and pushed it under the china cabinet but Daddy acted as if he hadn't seen me. He went out the door and slammed it. Then he got into his car and left.

I ran into the kitchen to see Mommy. She was crying.

This went on for days and days. Nancy was sad, too, and when we'd hear Mommy and Daddy talking loud in the night, she'd cry. I tried every way I could to make them laugh so things would be like before. Then one day I woke up from a nap and saw Mommy and Nancy standing by the door with their bags.

Were they going away? I ran to them. Mommy picked me up and hugged me and I kissed her nose. Then she handed me to Nancy and she also hugged me and I kissed her nose, too. They were leaving and I knew it wasn't like going to the store or to school. This was different and very sad. I cried a little.

Suddenly, I was all alone in the house and the ticking of the
hall clock sounded so loud! I was scared. Would Daddy come
home or had he left, too. Would I be left all alone to live in the
house by myself? Who would get my food and play with me?
I waited with Mr. Bear there in the dark by the front door.

After a while Mr. Bear asked me to tell him how I was feeling. He said the most important thing is to tell someone when you're sad, or lonely, or scared. So we talked about it for a very long time. I didn't know how but I knew that things were going to be different in our lives unless Mommy and Nancy returned.

It was later than usual when Daddy came home because the
street lights had come on and I could no longer see the sailboats
in the sea. He picked up the note on the table that said "goodbye"
and stared at it for a very long time. Then he looked into the
empty closets in Mommy and Nancy's rooms. I felt so very sad.

Daddy was sad, too. He hugged me and I gave him lots of kisses. After we had our dinner, I expected him to play "go fetch" with me as he did most every night. I went and got the ball but he just sat there in his chair staring off into space. I could tell he wasn't intersted in playing ball.

I went and got Mr. Bear and brought him to Daddy. He let us
sit in his lap and watch television. That night he let me and
Mr. Bear sleep on his bed but the next few days were an unhappy
time. Daddy seldom smiled and hardly said a word to me. For
several days he left me home with just Mr. Bear for company.

Finally, one night, while sitting on his lap watching television I
decided to take Mr. Bear's advice and tell Daddy just how lonely
it was being in the house all day without any people around.
And, you know, it worked! He called me his "baby" and played
with me for the first time since Mommy and Nancy left.

It was after that he started taking me to work with him. Daddy had a very large office all of his own and I had fun exploring it. It was an exciting new world for me. Once, when he was out of the office, I jumped onto his chair and then onto his desk and sat on some important papers he'd been going over with his pen.

I guess I must have dozed off to sleep because the next thing I knew, I heard people laughing. I opened my eyes to see Daddy and his secretary, Mrs. Spencer, smiling at me. "Oh, look!" Mrs. Spencer said, "Lacey is keeping guard over those valuable contracts for you!" That made me feel very important.

There were lots of people at Daddy's company to be friends with. Sometimes, when Daddy was busy, one of the people in the office would play go fetch with me or take me for a walk in the park. It was fun to chase the ball on the soft grass. Before long I had all sorts of friends and I started having fun again.

Daddy started smiling more, too. The days got longer and as
time went on we could go for long walks along the beach after
work. I loved being chased by the water when the waves came
in. At first I'd get my feet wet but I soon learned how to run
faster than the waves that rushed at me across the wet sand.

One Sunday afternoon Nancy came to visit. I was so happy to see her! We played together for hours and then Daddy took us for a ride in his automobile. Of course, by that time I was used to riding in cars. What I liked best about the ride was Daddy stopped and bought us very large ice cream cones.

I really hated saying goodbye to Nancy. Mommy came to pick her up in a car and I got to play with her for a few minutes. She and Daddy were very polite to each other and didn't talk loud the way they'd done before Mommy moved away. After seeing the three of them together again, I began to understand.

It seems that sometimes adults find they can't live together anymore. And if you're part of their family you have to live one place or another and live apart from one of them. That doesn't mean the one who goes away loves you any less. I realized that Daddy still loved Nancy, and that Mommy still loved me.

After that I began to see that Mr. Bear was right. It takes
time for everyone to get used to the idea of living apart.
Just because you don't live with some of your family
all the time doesn't mean they've stopped loving you, or
that you have to stop loving them.

That was an important lesson for me to learn. I could be happy living with Daddy in the pretty house by the sea, and Nancy could be happy living with Mommy in their cozy apartment across from the park. That way we both would always have someone very special to visit.

I've made lots and lots of new friends, and I have people to play with every day, and when Daddy has to go out of town on business I get to stay with Mommy and Nancy and we have fun. I hardly ever get lonely or feel sad anymore. But when I do, I remember what Mr. Bear told me to do.

I talk to someone and tell them how I'm feeling. I certainly
hope you always remember Mr. Bear's advice. Everyone has
days when they are a little sad, or scared, or lonely and it really
does make you feel better to tell someone about it. Who do you
talk to when you feel like that?

Even though I can't be with you, I'd like for you to think of me as your special friend because we should all care about each other. All you have to do when you're feeling sad is make believe I am right there with you, giving you big kisses on your nose, while you're telling me about your problems.

Miles and miles may separate us but there is a way we can keep in touch. The mailman! I know some dogs are supposed to have problems with the mailman but I'm certainly not one of them. If you want to write and tell me about yourself or things that bother you, just address the envelope this way:

It is very important that you remember you are a special person, and my friend. Don't ever forget that, and always remember someone loves you a lot and Lacey would like to hear from you. All you have to do is send me a letter. And I'll answer you and send you my love in return.